TO ALL THE GRANDPARENTS
NEVER AFRAID TO BE SILLY,
ESPECIALLY PAPA TERRY

**www.mascotbooks.com**

*Chicken Lips*

**For more information, please contact:**
Mascot Books
620 Herndon Parkway #320
Herndon, VA 20170
info@mascotbooks.com

Second Printing. This Mascot Books edition printed in 2019.

Library of Congress Control Number: 2018905957

CPSIA Code: PRT0219B
ISBN-13: 978-1-68401-878-9

Printed in the United States

# CHICKEN LIPS

BY KRISTY HAMBY

ILLUSTRATED BY MARIANELLA AGUIRRE

# THIS IS CHICKEN LIPS.

Yes, you heard that right, CHICKEN LIPS the cow!

Chicken Lips was the most energetic calf the farmer had ever seen. He liked swinging his head back and forth so the bell around his neck chimed, and he loved doing giant belly-flops into the pond. But there was one thing Chicken Lips did not like...

...his name. All the other cows gave him a hard time about it.

"What kind of name is Chicken Lips for a cow?" they cried. "What does that even mean? Chickens don't have lips!"

Then they laughed and laughed at him.

Chicken Lips was determined to figure out why he had such a goofy name, so he set off in search of answers.

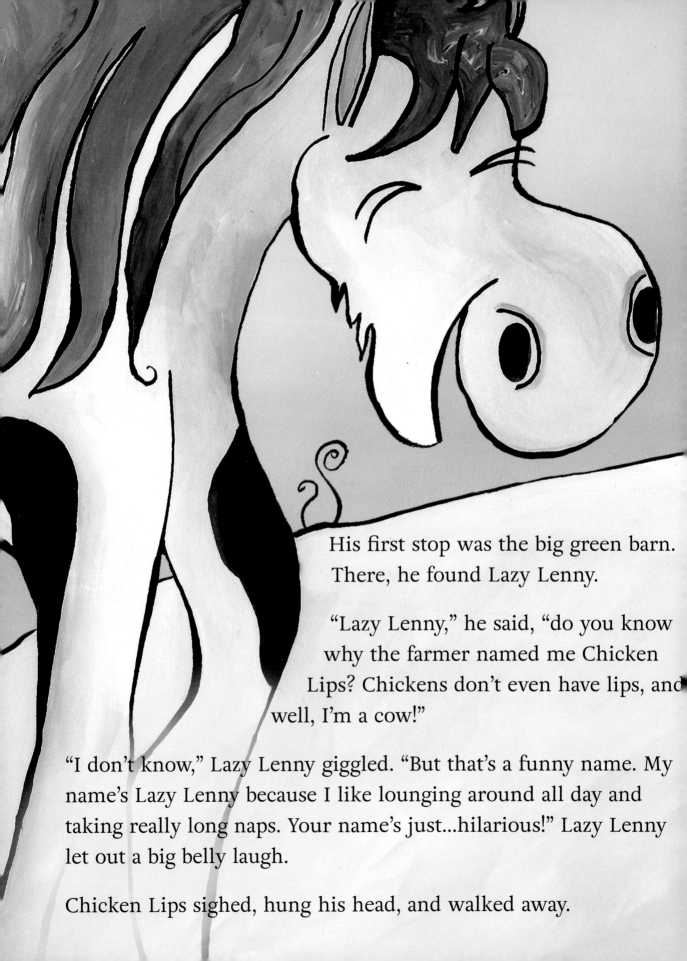

His first stop was the big green barn.
There, he found Lazy Lenny.

"Lazy Lenny," he said, "do you know
why the farmer named me Chicken
Lips? Chickens don't even have lips, and
well, I'm a cow!"

"I don't know," Lazy Lenny giggled. "But that's a funny name. My
name's Lazy Lenny because I like lounging around all day and
taking really long naps. Your name's just...hilarious!" Lazy Lenny
let out a big belly laugh.

Chicken Lips sighed, hung his head, and walked away.

Next, he went to see the old, wise sheep. "Fluffy," he said, "do you know why the farmer named me, *a cow*, Chicken Lips?"

The kind sheep smiled and said, "I don't know why the farmer named you that, but I'm sure he had a good reason. My name's Fluffy because of all the soft wool I provide. The farmer always picks good names for his animals, don't you worry."

**"BUT I AM WORRIED,"** said Chicken Lips as he walked away.

Chicken Lips didn't know where to go next. So he stomped in a nearby mud puddle. Then he flicked his big ears back and forth like he was playing peek-a-boo. Then he chased his tail around in big, silly circles.

"WHERE'D YOU LEARN TO DO THAT?" asked the farmer's dog.

"Oh, hey Round Up. I learned it from you. Can you help me with something else?"

"What's that?' asked Round Up.

"You don't know why the farmer named me Chicken Lips, do you?"

"Nope," said Round Up, laughing, "but it sure is a silly name. My name's Round Up because I keep all the sheep in line. Maybe you could ask the chickens?"

"Great idea!" said Chicken Lips, then he barreled off to the chicken coop. Surely his namesake would have the answer!

"Miss Feathers," Chicken Lips said, "you're a chicken. Do you know why the farmer named me, *a cow*, Chicken Lips?"

"**HMPH!** I most certainly do not!" she said. "Chickens are special animals, and you are definitely not one. You don't even have feathers!"

"I know," said Chicken Lips, feeling his worst.

Chicken Lips was trudging away from the chicken coop
when he heard his favorite noise. The farmer's old truck!
It was treat time! Not even Chicken Lips's silly name could
stop him from enjoying his favorite snack: POPCORN.
He ran as fast as he could to the truck.

**"LOOK! IT'S CHICKEN LIPS!"** cried the farmer's granddaughters. "Look how funny he runs!"

They laughed and laughed as Chicken Lips raced his way to the farmer for some popcorn.

"Hey there, Chicken Lips!" the farmer cried. "Don't you just love the taste of popcorn? Here you go!"

While Chicken Lips snacked away, one of the girls asked, "Papa, why'd you name our cow Chicken Lips?"

"Chickens don't even have lips," said the other.

The farmer smiled. "Well," he said, "Chicken Lips is the most playful, bouncy cow I have ever seen, and he deserved to have a special name."

"And I knew he was your most favorite of all the cows," continued the farmer, "so I knew he needed a name that would make you two laugh because that is my most favorite sound in the whole world!"

"We love the name Chicken Lips, and we love you too, Papa!" the girls said, laughing. "He really is our favorite friend on the farm!"

Chicken Lips beamed! He couldn't believe his ears! What a lucky cow he was with a very special name! After all, there's only one

# CHICKEN LIPS!

# ABOUT THE AUTHOR

Kristy Hamby can trace her love of writing back to her wonderful first grade teacher. That love has stayed with her through the years and inspired her to write her first children's book about her real-life oddly named cow, Chicken Lips.

Kristy enjoys watching Chicken Lips play with his herd in the beautiful pastures of north Georgia where she resides with her husband and three spirited kids. She is a stay-at-home mom who loves reading, writing, baking, playing piano (church hymnals are her favorite!), and watching her son play baseball.